First Little Readers™

L

Sloth Can't Sleep

by Liza Charlesworth

ISBN: 978-1-338-89048-8

Designer: Cynthia Ng; Illustrated by John Lund

Copyright © 2023 by Liza Charlesworth. All rights reserved. Published by Scholastic Inc.

1 2 3 4 5 6 7 8 9 10   68   31 30 29 28 27 26 25 24 23 22

Printed in Jiaxing, China. First printing, January 2023.

Deep in the rain forest
lived a furry creature named Sloth.
Sloth made his home in a tall green tree
with his pals Frog, Lizard, and Snake.

Sloth needed A LOT of sleep.
He snoozed 20 hours a day.
"*ZZZZZZZZZZZZZZZZZZZZZZZZZZ!*"
But his pals did NOT need a lot of sleep.
They always wanted him to play!

"Get up and jump with me!" said Frog.
"Nope," said Sloth. "I need to sleep."

"Get up and scurry with me!" said Lizard.
"Nope," said Sloth. "I need to sleep."

"Get up and climb with me!" said Snake.
"Nope," said Sloth. "I need to sleep."

Then, Sloth closed his big round eyes
and he snoozed and snoozed.
"*ZZZZZZZZZZZZZZZZZZZZZZZZZZ!*"
"Oh, well," said his pals.

One night, Frog, Lizard, and Snake
decided to stay up ALL NIGHT LONG.
"Will you stay up with us, too?"
they asked Sloth hopefully.
"Nope," replied Sloth. "I need to sleep."

But Sloth did NOT sleep
a single wink. Why?
His pals talked and giggled.

They munched on popcorn.
They played games and music.
They were LOUD, LOUD, LOUD!

9

"CAN YOU PLEASE BE QUIET!" shouted Sloth.
"YOU KNOW I NEED TO SLEEP!"
That made Frog and Lizard
and Snake feel really bad.
"We're sorry!" they said.

"We'll stay up ALL NIGHT LONG
in the tall tree next door!"
Jump, scurry, slide.
Off went Frog and
Lizard and Snake.

Now, Sloth couldn't hear a peep
from Frog and Lizard and Snake.
But he still wasn't able to sleep.
Why? Because it was way TOO quiet.
Plus, Sloth missed his friends a lot.

So Sloth hollered, "COME BACK, GUYS!
"I'VE DECIDED TO STAY UP ALL NIGHT LONG, TOO!"
"YIPPEE SKIPPY!" they yelled with glee.
Back came Frog and Lizard and Snake.
Jump, scurry, slide.

Sloth had a blast with his pals.
They munched on popcorn.
They played games and giggled.
They sang and danced.
It was fun, fun, fun!

But all that fun made them tired.
So NO ONE stayed up all night.
Frog fell asleep.
And Lizard fell asleep.
And Snake fell asleep.

And Sloth closed his eyes, too.
Then, he and his friends all snoozed happily
in that tall green tree under the moon.
"*ZZZZZZZZZZZZZZZZZZZZZZZZZ!*"